The Baron's Hunting Party

A counting story by Sally Kilroy

Viking Kestrel

Baron Bertie lives in the hill country. He has **one wife** called Georgina. As a special treat, he brings her breakfast in bed every Tuesday.

Bertie is usually very brave,
but he is afraid of mice.

The Baron's **two children**, James and Alice, like to play jokes on him at breakfast time when he is least expecting it.

2 children

Gruff, who claims that
he is the best guard dog,

Bertie has **three dogs**. He only wanted one dog, but when he went to collect a puppy, he liked them all…

Casper, who does tricks to get his master's attention,

and Quincy, who says he loves his master best.

3 dogs

Baron Bertie's home is a large castle with **four towers**. The first tower carries the flag-pole. The second is used by the Baron's soldiers to practise escape drill. The third has the guard-room on top of it. And the fourth is being repaired by the Bashwell Brothers, who are rather accident-prone.

Sir Oswald's castle only has two towers.

ARGH!

NOT AGAIN

4 towers

As well as the family, there are **five servants**...

a cook who knows that he cooks the very tastiest dishes, but still likes to make sure,

a kitchen-maid who can't help being a bit clumsy,

5 servant

a footman to help the Baron have his bubble bath, and to find his riding boots, which he is always losing,

TUM TE TUM!

a lady-in-waiting to brush the Baroness's hair, which reaches down to her waist,

RIP ROARING ROMANCES

and last but not least, a jolly jester to tell everyone funny jokes.

Jolly Jokes

Bertie also has **six soldiers**, to march about the battlements and guard the castle. Their names all begin with 'H', to make it easier for Bertie to remember them...

Sir Oswald,

Cuthbert,
Sir Oswald's son
who is supposed
to be very clever

:o go on a hunting expedition…

Roger,

Bernard,

DID I EVER TELL YOU THE ONE ABOUT THE PINK GOOSE?

Duncan, who plays in the village band,

Percy,

and Fergus, who was not a good rider and hoped that he wouldn't fall off.

7 friends

They saddled **eight horses** and off they went.

Cuthbert fell off when his saddle slipped round. His horse got quite a fright.

8 horses

Meanwhile, things were busy back at the castle. Cook was preparing for the evening's banquet.

11 eggs

"I'm sure there were **twelve oranges** just now…"

12 oranges

The Baroness and some of the other ladies were trying to finish a new wall-hanging for the great hall.

"That's **thirteen boars' heads** embroidered. Only one more to do…"

13 **boars' heads**

The jester was in a complete muddle after looking through **seventeen books** for jokes.

17 **books**

At last the hunting party returned.

"Look what we've caught, my dea[r]

The boar ran amok through the kitchen before escaping

"ghteen animals," said Bertie.

PHEW!

..I SAY..

The children decided to let the three rabbits out of the cage, but all the other animals escaped at the same time.

18 animals

The hunters had a bath, and then they all sat down to a huge banquet. They were so hungry that they ate **nineteen dishes** of food.

19 dishes

It had all been too much for Cuthbert.

Luckily the castle had lots of rooms, so they could all stay the night and sleep off the feast. The footman managed to find **twenty hot-water bottles**.

20 hot-water bottles

"SNAP!" The night watch were playing cards.

SNORE!
SNORE!

"Yum!" The cook couldn't resist finishing off the cake.

VIKING KESTREL

Puffin Books, Penguin Books Ltd, Harmondsworth, Middlesex, England
Viking Penguin Inc., 40 West 23rd Street, New York, New York 10010, U.S.A.
Penguin Books Australia Ltd, Ringwood, Victoria, Australia
Penguin Books Canada Limited, 2801 John Street, Markham, Ontario, Canada L3R 1B4
Penguin Books (N.Z.) Ltd, 182-190 Wairau Road, Auckland 10, New Zealand

First published 1987

Typeset in Century Schoolbook.
Printed in Hong Kong
by Imago Publishing Limited
British Library Cataloguing in Publication Data available
ISBN 0-670-81313-3